SACRAMENTO PUBLIC LIBRARY

3 3029 04577 7349

D0459265

FAIR OAKS LIBRARY
11601 FAIR OAKS BOULEVARD
FAIR OAKS, CA 95628
DEC - 2001

Feathers, Flaps, & Flops

FABULOUS EARLY FLIERS

by Bo Zaunders

illustrated by Roxie Munro

Dutton Children's Books · New York

To Robert E. Munro, who learned to fly late in life

—B.Z. & R.M.

Text copyright © 2001 by Bo Zaunders
Illustrations copyright © 2001 by Roxie Munro
All rights reserved.

CIP Data is available.

Published in the United States 2001 by Dutton Children's Books,
a division of Penguin Putnam Books for Young Readers
345 Hudson Street, New York, New York 10014
www.penguinputnam.com
Designed by Richard Amari
Printed in Hong Kong
First Edition
10 9 8 7 6 5 4 3 2 1
ISBN 0-525-46466-2

Contents

Introduction

In 1507, John Damian, an Italian living in Scotland, made himself a pair of feathered wings and jumped off the wall of Stirling Castle in the Scottish Highlands. His destination: France. But instead of reaching that distant country some four hundred miles away, he plunged straight into a pile of manure and broke his thighbone. Many so-called "birdmen" before and after him had tried to fly on homemade wings and failed just as miserably. But none of them had Damian's ready explanation for lack of success.

"I shouldn't have used chicken feathers," he said. "After all, chickens don't fly. They're ground birds with a natural attraction to common soil. Had my wings been made of eagle's feathers, I could have easily made it to France." Not much more is known about Damian except that he didn't attempt to fly again.

Throughout history, people have gone to extraordinary lengths pursuing the dream of human flight. Several monks—the dreamers and the intellectuals of the Middle Ages—risked life and limb plummeting from various abbeys and church towers. Obsessed with the challenge, the Renaissance genius Leonardo da Vinci—painter, sculptor, architect, scientist, and a contemporary of Damian—filled hundreds of pages with sketches of flying machines. Earlier there were such semimythical would-be fliers as Bladud, the ninth king of Britain, and King Kavus, who ruled Persia around 1500 B.C. The former "brake his necke as from a Towre he thot to scale the Sky." King Kavus gives us history's first carrot-and-stick story. To a throne of wood and gold on which four starved eagles were strapped, he attached long poles hung with legs of mutton. When the birds flapped frantically to get to the meat, they lifted the royal seat into the air. Soon, however, they grew tired and dropped His Majesty in a nearby forest. Humiliated, King Kavus decided that human beings were not meant to fly. Ever after, he was known as the Foolish King.

But, of course, human limitation did not apply to the gods. Flying has been a popular theme in mythology. Hermes, a Greek god, "flew as fleet as thought" with wings on his sandals and helmet; the Scandinavian Thor thundered through the skies in a chariot drawn by goats; the people of Easter Island have Makemake, half human, half bird.

When invading the heavens, the province of the gods, humans were likely to be punished. In the classic Greek tale of Daedalus and his son Icarus, Icarus ignores his father's warning not to fly too close to the sun. In consequence, the wax holding together Icarus's homemade wings melts, and he plunges to his death in a part of the Mediterranean now called the Icarian Sea.

It took a long time before flight became a reality. As visionary and brilliant as da Vinci's proposed flying machines were five hundred years ago, they would never fly because of one fatal flaw: They depended on muscle power without taking into account the enormous difference between a person and a bird. To fly like a bird, a person would need a six-foot chest to accommodate the required muscles.

Before the Wright brothers invented the airplane in 1903, there were kites and balloons. In the Far East, people flew kites and kites flew people before the birth of Christ. There, many centuries ago, kites reached such large sizes they could be used for, among other things, spying on enemies and landing soldiers in besieged cities. Like the airplane, the hot-air balloon was invented by two brothers, Joseph-Michel and Jacques-Étienne Montgolfier. That same year, 1783, the first hydrogen balloon was launched, and an era of balloonmania was born. Fashionable people had miniature balloons painted on their buttons and snuffboxes. In 1785, Jean-Pierre Blanchard, a Frenchman, and Dr. John Jeffries, an exiled American, set out from England in an attempt to

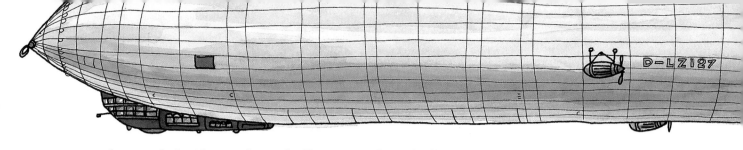

cross the English Channel in a balloon. As their balloon lost altitude, they lightened the load by throwing things out, including a bottle of cognac, their jackets, and finally their "trowsers." After a rough-and-tumble, two-hour voyage they landed in France on top of a tree, chilled to the bone but happy to have made it. Now, over two hundred years later, balloons still go anywhere the wind takes them. Which, as was proven in 1999 by Bertrand Piccard and Brian Jones, can be around the world.

Also before airplanes came dirigibles—steerable balloons with engines. From their invention at the turn of the century, dirigibles evolved into the mammoth *Graf Zeppelin,* a 776-foot-long, rigid airship, which in the late 1920s and '30s shuttled mail and people across the Atlantic. The gondola below carrried only twenty passengers and, with a crew of nearly fifty, was rather like a luxury ocean liner. Passengers dined at tables set with linen and silver, slept in commodious staterooms, and strolled along a promenade deck with a gorgeous view of the earth and ocean below. All this ended in 1937. As the *Hindenburg,* a sister ship, started to land in America, its hydrogen-filled interior burst into flames. Thirty-five people were killed. These dinosaurs of the skies are now gone. Blimps, using helium instead of highly inflammable hydrogen, have taken their place.

On December 17, 1903, a fragile craft, constructed of wood, baling wire, and muslin cloth, lifted into the air and flew for twelve seconds across the sands of Kill Devil Hill on the Outer Banks of North Carolina. It may not seem like much now, but it was, as the pilot, Orville Wright, said, "the first time in the history of the world in which a machine carrying a man had raised itself by its own power into the air in full flight." What had eluded scientific minds for centuries—heavier-than-air flight—had finally become a reality, thanks to Wilbur and Orville Wright, two bicycle mechanics from Dayton, Ohio.

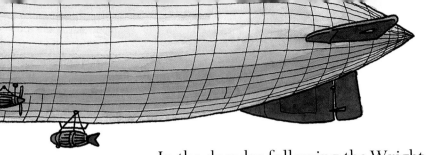

In the decades following the Wright brothers' tentative first hop, aviation remained fraught with danger. After the dreamers and inventors came the men and women who, against staggering odds, risked their lives. Many were looking for new records to break. Most people have heard of Charles Lindbergh and Amelia Earhart, but they were only two in a long line of pioneer pilots. In 1909, a Frenchman, Louis Blériot, winged across the English Channel. Two years later, Cal Rodgers set out to span the American continent in a series of short hops. Although the first to do it alone, Lindbergh was not the only one to conquer the North Atlantic. Eight years earlier, in 1919, two Englishmen, John Alcock and Arthur Whitten Brown, had flown from Newfoundland to Ireland nonstop—a hair-raising adventure in which Brown, the navigator, in the subzero temperature of high altitude, climbed out on top of the fuselage to remove ice covering the fuel dial.

Daredevils and barnstormers dominated the 1920s. Hazardous air races were the rage in the 1930s. But it was also the decade during which aviation became safer and more reliable. The 1930s marked the beginning of airlines and regular airmail service. Since then, our ancient dream of flying has been realized beyond our wildest imagination. In 1947, Chuck Yeager, an American, broke the sound barrier; ten years later, the Russians launched *Sputnik I*. It was the first passenger-carrying object ever hurled into space. As the Montgolfier brothers had done two centuries earlier, the Russians turned to the animal kingdom for choice of passenger—in their case Laika, a dog.

When, in 1969, Neil Armstrong stepped onto the Moon's Sea of Tranquillity, he carried with him a small piece of linen from the Wright brothers' original flier. It was a fitting tribute to those bold, even reckless people who persevered for the thrill, as Beryl Markham put it, of that "momentary escape from the eternal custody of earth."

THE MONTGOLFIER BROTHERS

*E*veryone at Louis XVI's magnificent château in Versailles clamored for a good view. Spectators crammed the windows and filled the rooftops. In the courtyard below, amidst the milling, jostling crowd, a huge, multicolored cloth stirred and rose, apparently on its own. It was September 19, 1783. Some 130,000 people watched with excitement as the first free-flying, hot-air balloon ever to carry living creatures was about to be launched. The passengers: a sheep, a duck, and a rooster.

Off it went, this small menagerie. The king, as curious as anyone, watched the flight through field glasses. When the balloon came down just two miles away, he turned to one of its inventors, Étienne Montgolfier, and said, *"Magnifique! But now we must find out if the animals survived."*

9

When picked up by the king's men, the sheep, duck, and rooster proved to be in excellent condition. In a letter to his wife that evening, an exultant Étienne playfully quoted the three as saying, "We feel fine. We've landed safely despite the wind. It's given us an appetite." In his own voice, Étienne continued, "That is all we could gather from the talk of the three travelers, seeing that they don't know how to write and that we have neglected to teach them French. The first could say only *'Quack, Quack'*; the second, *'Cock-a-doodle-do'*; and the third, no doubt a member of the Lamb family, replied only *'Baa'* to all our questions."

It had been a long, exciting day. Before drifting off to sleep, a happy Étienne chuckled to himself as he recalled his brother Joseph-Michel's reaction to the choice of animal passengers. "Try to take a cow," he had written. "That will create an extraordinary effect, far more than a panicky sheep that no one will be able to see." Dear old Joseph. It was he who had started it all with that urgent and rather perplexing note ten months ago. . .

Back then, Étienne lived in the small town of Annonay in southern France, managing the family's papermaking factory. Joseph, older by five years, lived in a neighboring city, Avignon, where he spent most of his time reading books on physics and conducting experiments. An amateur scientist, Joseph had been ruminating in front of his fireplace one evening, questioning whether the "gas" that whisked the smoke, sparks, and pieces of charred paper up the chimney could be made to lift solid, man-made objects. Anxious to find out, he set to work right there in the room, constructing a lightweight, boxlike frame of thin wooden slats. Around it he stretched silk taffeta, leaving a one-foot-square opening at the bottom. Resting the box on a support, he inserted scraps of paper through the opening and ignited them. In seconds, the contraption rose and bumped against the ceiling—dumbfounding his landlady, who happened to be present.

Excited, Joseph dashed off a note to his favorite younger brother: "Get in a supply of taffeta and cordage, quickly, and you'll see one of the most astonishing sights in the world."

A few days later in a field outside Annonay, with Étienne as an enthusiastic audience, Joseph launched yet another "little box," which soared to seventy feet and floated in the air for a full minute. Together the brothers built larger models, modifying the original design to the spherical shape of a classical balloon.

On June 5, after much experimentation, they staged a public demonstration with a balloon made of coarsely woven fabric layered with paper. As the hot air from a small fire filled the limp bag, it swelled into a bulging globe, thirty-five feet wide, and, to the townspeople's utter amazement, shot straight into the sky. It ascended to a height of a thousand feet and rode on the air currents for over a mile. Not since Creation, the people thought, had there been such a miracle.

Word of the demonstration reached Paris, where a scientist, J. A. C. Charles, soon developed a different kind of balloon, using hydrogen gas instead of hot air. On account of his successful launch of a much smaller balloon—eighteen feet in diameter—and the June 5 launch of the Montgolfier brothers, balloons became the hot topic throughout the country. Particularly impressed by the Montgolfier accomplishment, the king ordered a command performance at Versailles—the one that would launch the sheep, the duck, and the rooster.

Only Étienne should go, the family decided. Joseph was too shy and unworldly for such an important mission. Before Étienne left, their father, predicting that human flight would come next, made one condition: His sons must swear an oath never to fly any of their perilous machines themselves. That would be left for two other men to do—in Paris on November 21, 1783.

All Paris came out to watch this Montgolfier balloon—seven stories high and decorated with golden suns, the signs of the zodiac, and the king's monogram. The king doubted that people would survive balloon flight, so he suggested that two criminals under sentence of death be used for the experiment. Pilâtre de Rozier, a young scientist, protested vehemently. Why should, as he put it, "two vile criminals have the first glory of rising to the sky?" He volunteered, along with his aristocratic friend, Marquis d'Arlandes.

Up went this incredible object. It was a fearsome sight; many were on their knees, praying. As a hushed silence prevailed throughout the city, the voices of the two airborne voyagers could be heard quite clearly. Stationed on a circular platform at the bottom of the balloon, they joked and shouted commands at each other as they forked bundles of straw into the balloon's burner. A moment of panic! Sparks from the flames began eating holes in the fabric of their fragile craft. But the men were prepared—with buckets of water and sponges attached to long poles. Minutes later they were nearly skewered on a church tower. The flight lasted about twenty minutes. On landing, Pilâtre's coat caught fire. Fortunately, he wasn't wearing it.

Benjamin Franklin, the inventor and statesman who was America's ambassador to France at the time, watched the spectacle from his balcony. He had also witnessed both Charles's launch of the first hydrogen balloon and the flight of the Montgolfier balloon with its furred and feathered passengers. Someone once asked him, "Of what use is a balloon?"

"Sir," Franklin replied, "of what use is a newborn baby?"

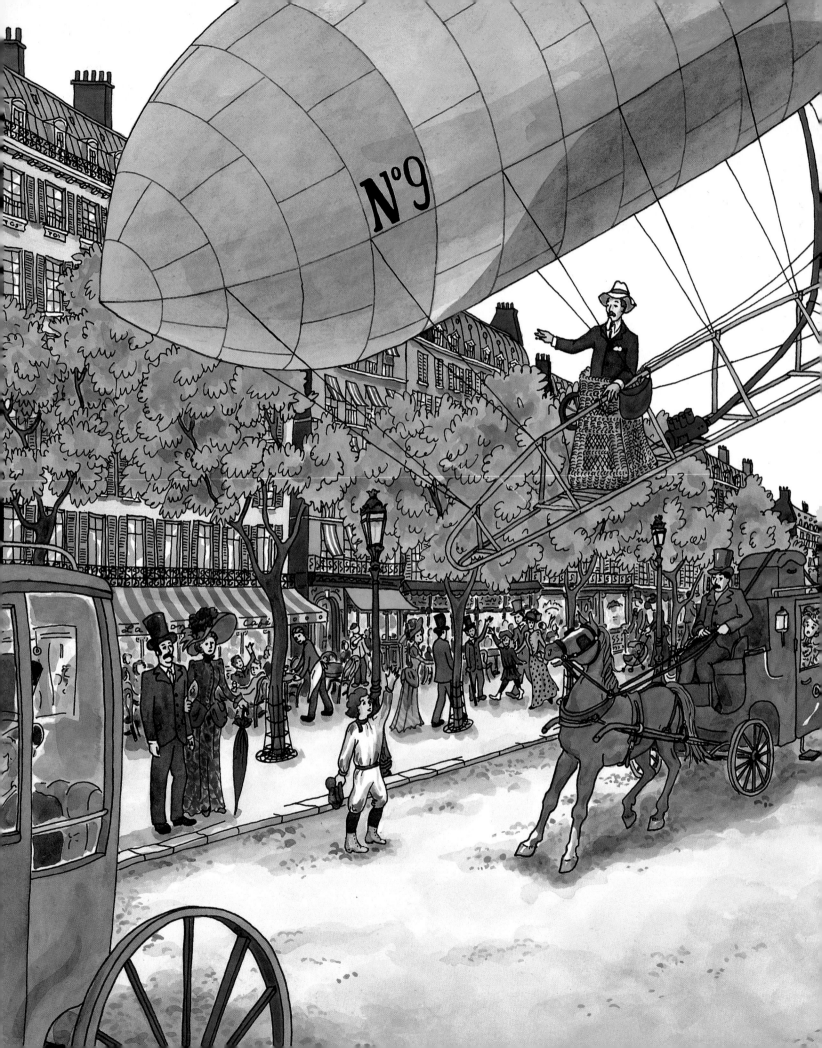

ALBERTO SANTOS-DUMONT

*H*orse-drawn carriages stopped dead in their tracks. People waved and pointed at the sky. "Look!" they shouted. "There's Santos in one of his flying machines!" Above them, along the Champs-Élysées, Paris's fashionable boulevard, sailed a strange-looking contraption: a cigar-shaped balloon under which was mounted a gasoline engine and a large propeller. Also suspended below, in a wicker basket, stood a dapper little man with a neatly trimmed mustache, starched collar, and Panama hat. Spotting an agreeable sidewalk café, he landed his airship in the street and hitched it to a lamppost. Then, as throngs of admirers gathered around him, he calmly ordered his morning cup of coffee. He was Alberto Santos-Dumont, a twenty-nine-year-old Brazilian aviator who, a year earlier, in the fall of 1901, had astounded the Parisians with one of the most spectacular feats in early aviation history.

15

In 1901, when controlled flight was yet to be mastered, a wealthy member of the new Paris Aero Club had set up a prize of 100,000 francs. The money was to go to the first pilot who took off from the club, circled the Eiffel Tower, and, covering a distance of seven miles, returned within thirty minutes. Alberto, who by then was building *No. 5*, his fifth dirigible—a steerable balloon powered by an engine—was determined to win the prize. The money meant little to him; the glory and the opportunity to "put over" his aeronautical ideas were everything.

Anyone except Alberto might have been discouraged by what happened. In his first attempt, just as he rounded the Eiffel Tower, his little 16-horsepower motor sputtered and conked out, causing him and his dirigible to fall into a tree. His second try, after the craft had been fixed, was even more disheartening. Gas began leaking, the wind was strong, and suddenly one of the suspension ropes holding his wicker basket snapped and caught the propeller. Cool as always, Alberto cut the engine and let the ship drift. With a loud noise, *No. 5* crashed onto the roof of the Trocadero Hotel and exploded, leaving the brave Brazilian suspended in his basket fifty feet above the ground. Along came the Paris fire department to cut him down. "My escape was narrow," admitted Alberto, more resolved than ever to continue with his quest.

Thousands of Parisians gathered along the flight path on October 19

to see Alberto make his third attempt in his new airship, *No. 6*. With a stiff wind at his back, he reached the tower and circled it in only nine minutes. Then, buffeted by gusts of wind, the airship swerved dangerously. Alberto regained control by shifting the ballast. At that point, the motor began acting up and nearly stopped. In order to fix it, Alberto had no choice but to leave the steering wheel and walk along a narrow undercarriage of struts and wires at the dizzying height of nearly a thousand feet. As he performed this human spider act and the craft resumed speed, the crowd went wild. People threw handkerchiefs and scarves into the air, and many men, in a befitting salute to the spin around the Eiffel Tower, whirled their hats on top of their walking sticks. "Did I make it?" shouted Alberto to the crowd below as he passed the finish line. *"Oui! Oui!"* the crowd roared back at him—and he had, with twenty-nine seconds to spare.

There was no one like "*le petit* Santos." He was the toast of Paris. Every time he appeared in public, people ran after him, shouting hurrahs or asking for his autograph. A starched collar was known as a Santos-Dumont collar; girls wore his picture on buttons and brooches.

A daredevil pilot and millionaire dandy—the family coffee estate had left him with a fortune—Alberto was also a hard worker who won the hearts of craftsmen; he was good at doing many of the things they did themselves. Building and perfecting dirigibles in his workshop, he had to be a mechanic, electrician, tailor, and blacksmith, all rolled into one.

Even as a boy growing up in Brazil, Alberto had been fascinated with things mechanical and with the idea of one day being able to fly. Arriving in Paris at eighteen, he became one of the first people to invest in a gasoline-driven automobile—in which he roamed the countryside at the then fabulous speed of fifteen miles an hour. From the Montgolfier brothers on, ballooning had been a popular sport among the rich. Trying it out, Alberto was immediately hooked and ordered a balloon made to his specifications. It was the world's smallest—large enough to carry his pint-size figure, yet so tiny it could be packed into a travel bag when not in use.

But a balloon goes only where the wind takes it—which was not necessarily where Alberto wanted to go. So he turned to what, in the late 1890s, was a fledgling science: dirigibles—balloons powered by engines and capable of being steered.

Steam engines had been tried but proved too heavy and not powerful enough. Alberto owned a motorized tricycle. Perhaps its little gasoline engine would do the trick. To make sure the vibrations from the engine, when airborne, would not shake the balloon to pieces, Alberto brought the tricycle to a large tree. There, with the help of his manservant, he slung it over a sturdy, low-hanging branch, climbed into the driver's seat, and started the engine. The vibrations were minimal—the tree barely shook—so the next step was to hook it under a balloon. This became airship *No. 1*, which led to *No. 2*, and so on.

Progress was not smooth. The cigar-shaped body of *No. 1* practically folded on its first run; *No. 2* smashed into a tree; *No. 3* experienced a rudder failure.

But, little by little, "my family," as Alberto called his growing number of airships, kept improving. He made fourteen altogether. *No. 4*, incidentally, had a bicycle saddle instead of a basket, handlebars for steering, and pedals for controlling the engine.

In 1906, inspired by reports of the Wright brothers' historic first flight in a heavier-than-air craft three years earlier, Alberto built his own airplane. Named *The Infuriated Grasshopper,* it looked like a bunch of boxes haphazardly thrown together. But it flew—only thirty-six feet, but far enough to establish Alberto as the first man in Europe to fly a heavier-than-air machine.

His final triumph in aircraft design was a plane with a wingspan of less than twenty feet. Made of bamboo, aluminum, and silk, it was so light that a strong man could lift it. Seeing him buzz around in it, people would shout delightedly, "Our Santos is riding a dragonfly!" And that's how the airplane got its name: *Demoiselle* (dragonfly). It was the fulfillment of Alberto's ultimate childhood dream of moving through space with perfect ease.

Alberto spent almost all his money on dirigibles and air-planes. He never patented any of them. These, he felt, were his gifts to aviation, from which everybody should be able to benefit. As for the prize money, after paying his crew of mechanics, he gave it to the poor of Paris.

Alberto Santos-Dumont loved everything high. His dining table in Paris had nine-foot legs with chairs to match. To reach it, the manservant climbed a short step stool. After retiring to Brazil, Alberto built a miniature house near the top of a steep hill—it looked like an airplane about to take off. He constructed it so that you could enter the house with your right foot only—"for luck," according to this remarkable little man.

CAL RODGERS

rs. John Heddy had just finished feeding her chickens when, out of the blue sky, whirled a dazzling white flying machine. Between the wings sat the pilot—tall, rawboned, with a cigar in his mouth. Having just been thrown off course by a willow tree tugging at his rear landing gear, he now saw power lines looming in his flight path. To avoid them, he cut the engine, hit another tree, and plunged into Mrs. Heddy's chicken coop.

Feathers floated as the pilot emerged from a tangle of wire, splintered wood, and torn fabric. Head bleeding, cigar still clenched between his teeth, he muttered, "My beautiful aeroplane! My beautiful aeroplane!"

His name was Cal Rodgers. His goal: to be the first man to fly across the United States.

20

It was 1911. Aviation was still in its infancy. Only eight years had elapsed since the Wright brothers had managed to stay airborne in a heavier-than-air machine. Less than 2 percent of the American people had ever seen an "aeroplane." Now and then, newspapers featured the exploit of some daredevil airman setting a new altitude or speed record—or crashing to his death. In the fall of 1910, the newspaper tycoon William Randolph Hearst had offered a $50,000 prize to the first pilot who flew across the American continent, coast to coast, in thirty days or less. Almost a year later, in September 1911, three men took up the challenge. One of them was Calbraith Perry Rodgers—or Cal, as he was known to family and friends.

Just three months earlier, Cal had never seen, much less flown, an airplane. When the navy sent his cousin John to Dayton to learn to fly a Wright plane, Cal followed him and took his first flying lesson. "He seemed to experience some sort of transformation," his cousin said, "as if he were about to sprout a pair of wings himself." After ninety minutes of instruction, Cal, who came from a well-to-do family, purchased his own plane. A month later he showed up in Chicago, where many of the world's best airmen were putting on a big, nine-day exhibition. There, to everyone's surprise, he won the grand prize for staying airborne longer than anyone else—a total of over twenty-seven hours, counting several flights. Proud of his physical stamina— necessary for long flights in the primitive planes of

that era—Cal was ready for the daunting task of the first transcontinental flight.

Cal knew that his venture would be far from simple. A special three-car train was rented to help him navigate through a country which, at that time, had no air routes and not a single airport. The train was paid for by a company that manufactured a grape drink named Vin Fiz. Part of the deal was that Cal would name his gleaming new Wright machine after the drink, decorate it with a cluster of grapes, and scatter leaflets from the sky. The train carried a second plane, plenty of spare parts, a crew of ten mechanics, Cal's wife, Mabel, his cousin John, his mother, and a host of reporters.

On September 17, Cal had a glorious takeoff from a racetrack at Sheepshead Bay in Brooklyn, New York. Heading for New Jersey, where the special train was waiting, Cal made a sensational sweep over Manhattan with "its deathtrap of tall buildings, spires, ragged roofs, and narrow streets," as one newspaper put it. It was, the writer continued, "a never-to-be-forgotten vision to all who were fortunate enough to see him." At his first stop, Middletown, New Jersey, an enormous crowd greeted Cal. Waiting also was Mabel, who, with all the others, had arrived by train. The next morning, less than a minute after liftoff, Cal plummeted into Mrs. Heddy's chicken coop.

Cal, his mechanics, and many of the citizens of Middletown immediately pitched in to rebuild the mangled *Vin Fiz*. A few days later, Cal was once again airborne, and happily so. "I was above the air currents going faster than the wind, and the engine was singing a sweet song. I lit a fresh cigar and let her go. . . ."

Past New York, over Pennsylvania and Ohio, into Indiana, the *Vin Fiz* buzzed on. Stopovers were frequent, as were brushes with death. Such a fragile craft (canvas and spruce held together by piano wire, and lacking windshield, armrest, and seat belt) was bound to cause problems. Taking off from Elmira, New York, Cal struck some telegraph wires and quickly had to settle back to earth for a few hours of repair. Shortly thereafter, a spark plug worked loose. Cal managed to hold it in place with one hand and fly the plane with the other until, disgusted with the situation, he decided to make an unscheduled landing. Near Salamanca, New York, he piled into a barbed-wire fence and demolished his plane for the second time. In early October, landing in Indiana, he was attacked by a bull. Airborne again, he found himself surrounded by lightning—making him the first pilot ever to fly in a thunderstorm. By the time he reached Chicago, the two other contenders had dropped out of the race, and Cal realized he was not going to make it to Los Angeles in thirty days. "Prize or no prize," he said to a reporter, "that's where I'm bound, and if canvas, steel, and wire together with a little brawn, tendon, and brain stick with me, I mean to get there."

So he pressed on. To avoid the Rocky Mountains, he turned south, flew all the way to Texas, then pushed west across New Mexico and Arizona—still U.S. territories in 1911. As he flew over California, a cylinder exploded, and metal shards punctured his left arm. The accident necessitated a two-hour operation but otherwise did little to slow down the intrepid aviator. At this point he had survived a dozen or so crashes, and his plane had been rebuilt so many times that only the rudder and a single strut remained of the original *Vin Fiz*.

On November 5, forty-nine days after leaving New York, Cal reached Los Angeles. Landing at Tournament Park in Pasadena, he was mobbed by twenty thousand cheering fans; he was wrapped in an American flag and driven around the field in a triumphant victory lap. Cal Rodgers had become a national hero. But for him it was not over until he had actually reached the Pacific Ocean.

Taking off for Long Beach, he crashed again and was hauled from the wreckage unconscious and with a broken ankle. A month later, walking with crutches, he hobbled back to the yet again rebuilt *Vin Fiz* for a second attempt. This time he succeeded. After he landed, he brought the plane to the water's edge, washing its wheels in the Pacific, and some fifty thousand spectators broke into thunderous applause.

"He will need every atom of courage in his makeup," Wilbur Wright had said of any man who attempted to win the Hearst prize. As well as an extraordinary measure of good luck, he might have added. Tragically, Cal's luck was about to run out. A few months later, taking his plane for a spin, he flew into a flock of seagulls and—just a few feet from where the *Vin Fiz* had so gloriously finished its cross-country trip—plunged to his death in the Long Beach surf.

BESSIE COLEMAN

Her silk scarf snapping in the slipstream, Bessie Coleman, the first black woman pilot, was plummeting straight to earth. After a series of stunts culminating in a flawless figure eight, her plane had climbed higher and higher until, alarmingly, the engine had stopped. Would this be the end of "Queen Bess," as she was known in the press? The spectators below froze with terror, then scattered in all directions.

Seconds before the inevitable crash, the coolheaded young aviator restarted the engine, swept over the heads of the awestruck crowd, and brought the plane in for a perfect landing. The seeming near tragedy had just been another one of Bessie's spine-tingling stunts.

Emerging from the cockpit, she broke into a dazzling smile. It was a sweet moment in Bessie's life. No one had thought she could ever become a pilot.

"Queen Bess," as the *Chicago Defender*, a prominent black newspaper, called her, had every reason to feel elated on this bright fall afternoon in 1922. Her dream to "amount to something one day" was coming true, despite overwhelming odds—being poor, black, and female.

Bessie Coleman was born in Texas in 1892, into a world of extreme poverty and deepening racial discrimination. Blacks could not vote and were restricted to all-black schools. Laws forbade them to use the same railroad cars, restaurants, rest rooms, and water fountains as whites. If they protested, they risked being whipped, tarred and feathered, even lynched. In 1900, when Bessie was eight, there were 115 lynchings in the South.

Bessie grew up in Waxahachie, thirty miles south of Dallas, where her father, a day laborer, had managed to scrape together enough money to buy a tiny plot of land. On it, he built a small house for his large family; Bessie had several older brothers and three younger sisters. In this climate of racial prejudice, being part Cherokee made the situation for Bessie's father particularly difficult. Unable to find work in Waxahachie, he tried to persuade his wife to go with him to Oklahoma, then Indian Territory. When she refused, he left without her. Bessie's mother began working as a domestic for a white family, leaving Bessie to care for her sisters.

Bessie didn't mind, except that it kept her away from school. She was a bright student, particularly good at math. At eighteen Bessie found work as a laundress. She saved every penny she could and, five years later, enrolled in a black college. There she became fascinated with aviation. She read about the Wright brothers, and, with special attention, about Harriet Quimby, a pioneer woman pilot. If only Bessie herself could fly! But poverty kept her from finishing even her first year of college. In 1915, Bessie left for Chicago, where two of her brothers lived, and landed a job as a manicurist at a barbershop on the city's South Side.

When she arrived, World War I was raging in Europe. In the *Chicago Defender*, Bessie read about Eugene Bullard, a young African-American pilot who had joined the French in their fight against the Germans. It thrilled her to imagine a black person flying an airplane. But it would take three more years and a chance remark before it occurred to Bessie that she herself might become a pilot. One day her brother John, who had served in the war, walked into the barbershop and began bragging about French women he had met. "Some," he boasted, "even fly airplanes."

"That's it," cried Bessie, electrified. "You just called it for me." Her mind was made up. But who would give her flying lessons? She approached a number of pilots, all white, all with the same reaction: "You're a Negro and a woman—you must be joking!" Undeterred, Bessie sought the advice of a valued customer in the barbershop, the publisher of the *Defender*. "Go to France," he said. "The French are much more accepting of both women and blacks—but, of course, first you have to learn the language."

That same day, Bessie began taking French lessons and, soon after, applied for a passport—giving her age as twenty-four instead of twenty-eight. She managed to get a better-paying job as the manager of a chili parlor, and a few months later she sailed for France. There she signed up with an aviation school. Her training included everything from banked turns and looping-the-loop to airplane mainte-

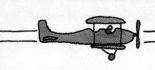

nance. She worked hard and, in the summer of 1921, became the first black woman to earn a pilot's license.

In the 1920s, there were no regular airlines. This was the decade of gypsy flying or, as it was also called, barnstorming. People paid to watch pilots perform thrilling, dangerous stunts. When Bessie returned to the United States, a dream slowly took shape. She would fly in air shows. With the money she earned, she would open a flight school for black people and, in her words, "give a little coloring" to aviation.

Back in the United States, an African-American woman pilot was big news. Thunderous applause and a rousing rendition of "The Star-Spangled Banner" greeted Bessie at her first air show on Long Island, New York. That performance led to bookings in Memphis, Tennessee, and, shortly, to the exhibition in Chicago. Bessie's future had never looked brighter. She managed to buy an old Curtiss Jenny, a favorite plane among barnstormers, and was all set for a performance in Los Angeles.

But, as Bessie flew to the airfield, the engine stalled, and she crashed into the street below. She was knocked unconscious, broke one leg, and fractured several ribs. From her hospital bed, distraught over having disappointed her fans, she sent a telegram to the local newspaper: TELL THEM THAT AS SOON AS I CAN WALK I'M GOING TO FLY! That was in February of 1923. By September she was back in a borrowed plane, performing to upbeat crowds in Columbus, Ohio. Shows in Texas and Florida followed. She became a frequent lecturer, speaking in churches and theaters, as well as at all-black schools.

30

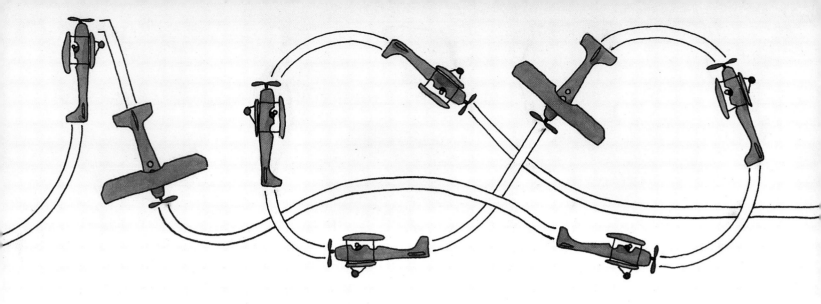

Bessie loved stunt flying and accepted its high risks. But her real ambition was a school. Sadly, she would never see that dream realized. In the summer of 1926, finally in possession of an airplane—another old run-down Jenny—Bessie was practicing parachuting with a pilot at the controls when a wrench slid into the gears and jammed the engine. The plane went into a spin and hurtled to earth. The other pilot was killed on impact; Bessie was thrown out of her seat and somersaulted several hundred feet to her death.

At a funeral service in Chicago, thousands of mourners paid their last respects to the brave young aviator. With her pluck and determination, Bessie Coleman had set an example for many black people. Although hampered throughout her life by poverty and prejudice—the planes she flew were always secondhand, and she was virtually ignored by the white newspapers—Bessie never allowed herself to become bitter.

"If I can create a minimum of my desires," she once told her family, "there shall be no regrets." Her dream of a flight school did not die. In 1929, one of her admirers, a successful black businessman and World War I veteran named William Powell, opened the Bessie Coleman Aero Club in Los Angeles. For decades it introduced young blacks to the world of aviation. Many have been inspired by the legacy left by Coleman—among them, Dr. Mae Jemison, the first woman African-American astronaut.

JIMMY DOOLITTLE

Some called it a "bumblebee," others called it a "flying milk bottle." Only seventeen feet long, with a chunky body and stubby wings, the Gee Bee Super Sportster looked like a toy airplane. It was the cutest little aircraft—and the deadliest. The Gee Bees were made for speed, not safety, and caused endless—often fatal—problems for their pilots. The perilous plane had only one undisputed master: Jimmy Doolittle.

In the 1932 Thompson Trophy race— aviation's Kentucky Derby—Doolittle, a celebrated test and race pilot, shattered a speed record as he whipped a Gee Bee around the racecourse at speeds averaging 252.6 miles per hour. Flying it, he commented, was a bit "like balancing a pencil on the tip of your finger."

32

The ultimate pilot—the Master of the Calculated Risk, as he was sometimes called—Jimmy Doolittle was a household name in America for some fifty years. His life and career coincide with the birth and development of flight in the United States. Born in 1896, he was seven when the Wright brothers took off from Kitty Hawk. He was around in the barnstorming days and in the era of the big air races that so thrilled people. As aviation advanced, so did Doolittle. His contribution toward greater air safety is now part of history, as is his raid against Tokyo during World War II. Yet this ultimate pilot grew up with no dreams of becoming a flier.

James H. Doolittle was born in California but spent his early childhood in Nome, a small gold-rush town on Alaska's west coast, where his father worked as a carpenter. Nome was a rough pioneer outpost thronged by thousands of prospectors in shacks and tents. Disputes were settled by guns, knives, and fists. A small boy with girlish locks, Jimmy was the natural target for bigger boys who delighted in pushing him around. Combative and a fierce fighter, the Doolittle boy soon gained their respect. At eight, he had his first glimpse of the outside world, visiting Seattle with his father. There he saw an automobile, a trolley car, and houses with paint on them.

In 1908, he and his mother moved to Los Angeles, while his father, hoping to find gold, stayed in Alaska. One reason for the move was to provide Jimmy with a better education. But the boy did not distinguish himself as a good student. Instead he was known for his swinging punch. At fifteen, he became the amateur bantamweight champion of the Pacific Coast—much to the distress of his mother, who hated the thought of her son turning into a boxer. Once, Jimmy got involved in a street riot and was hauled off to jail. "Keep him there until Monday morning," his mother told the police. "I'll come get him in time for school." A night in jail, she felt, might set him straight. It did. Never again, Jimmy vowed, would his emotions get the better of his reason.

About that time, Doolittle saw his first airplane and read an article in *Popular Mechanics* with instructions on how to build a Wright brothers' glider. Jimmy set to work, fashioning spruce wood into a pair of wings and covering them with cloth. The glider didn't fly. Neither did Santos's *Demoiselle,* his next *Popular Mechanics* project. But flying had now become an obsession, and in 1917, after completing two years of junior college, Jimmy enlisted in the U.S. Army, Aviation Section.

Height proved something of a problem. At five foot six, Jimmy could barely see out of the side of the plane in which he made his first flights. Still, proving to be a natural pilot, he was allowed to fly solo after only six hours of instruction. He had hoped to be sent overseas to fight in World War I. Instead, after basic training, he was picked as a flying instructor, soon earning a reputation for exceptional skill and daring. In 1922, granted the army's permission to try a transcontinental

flight, Doolittle flew from Florida to California in record time, finishing in less than twenty-four hours what it had taken Cal Rodgers nearly two months to accomplish eleven years earlier. The feat made Doolittle an instant celebrity. His ready grin and small cocky figure appeared on the front page of every newspaper. That same year, the army assigned him a job as a test pilot. Shortly thereafter, recognizing the value of an academic background to his practical experiments, Doolittle entered the Massachusetts Institute of Technology. School proved tough, but he stuck it out and, in 1925, emerged with a doctorate in aeronautical sciences. As both a scholar and a piloting genius, he was particularly valuable to a budding U.S. Air Force and was appointed head of a research team. Assignment: to solve the problem of flying in clouds or fog.

In those days, pilots had no instruments to guide them in bad weather. They relied on visibility. Doolittle, collaborating with a team of scientists, set to work. On September 24, 1929, after nearly a year of intense research, he conducted a demonstration that is now considered a milestone in aviation history—the first blind flight.

A hood was draped over the cockpit, blocking the view outside. Guided only by a special radio receiver and the glowing dials of some painstakingly designed instruments, Doolittle took off. He climbed to 1,000 feet, banked into a 180-degree turn, and, fifteen minutes later, landed a few feet from where he had started. He had seen neither sky nor air for the whole flight—only his instruments and the hood over the rear cockpit. It was not an especially dangerous flight—another pilot was seated in the front cockpit in case of an emergency—but it was an important breakthrough, proving once and for all the practicality of flying by instruments.

Jimmy had missed out on World War I, but he was not about to lose a chance to serve his country a quarter of a century later. When World War II broke out and the Japanese bombed Pearl Harbor, Doolittle, then a lieutenant colonel, was

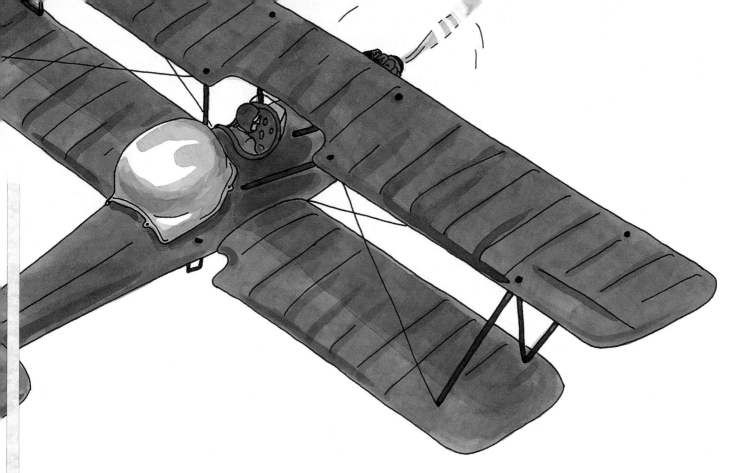

called to duty. His mission: to lead an attack on Tokyo in which, for the first time in history, bombers would be launched from an aircraft carrier. The now famous "Doolittle Raid," involving seventy-nine volunteers and sixteen bombers, took the Japanese by complete surprise. Although the raid caused relatively little damage, it was a turning point in the early stages of the war. In their darkest hour, the Americans and their allies had proved that the Japanese were neither unreachable nor invincible. DOOLITTLE DOO'OOD IT! one headline shouted.

Back in the United States, Doolittle was promoted to brigadier general and presented with the Congressional Medal of Honor. His career in aviation continued for many more years. He was now a celebrity, admired and respected not only in America but throughout the world. From a young boy who couldn't resist a fistfight, no matter what, Doolittle had come a long way. His cool, scientific approach to flying is now legendary. He was truly the Master of the Calculated Risk.

BERYL MARKHAM

She had taken off from Abingdon, England, and flown across Wales and the Irish Sea. It was already dark. Rain was falling. Below lay Ireland's west coast, with the flashing beam of the Berehaven Lighthouse—the "last light standing on the last land." Ahead stretched two thousand miles of unbroken ocean, most of which would have to be crossed in darkness. It was September 4, 1936. Beryl Markham was flying west with the night to America.

Several pilots had flown across the North Atlantic, west to east, aided by the prevailing tailwinds. Who would attempt to do it the other way—against the wind—from England? On a bet at a London dinner party a few months before, Beryl had accepted the challenge.

As she passed the lighthouse and flew out to sea, Beryl recalled a comment from the man who had furnished her with the plane: "Gee, I wouldn't tackle it for a million. Think of all that black water! Think of how cold it is!"

Beryl Markham was born in England in 1902. At age four, she moved with her divorced father to British East Africa (now Kenya), where he established a large farm to breed and train horses. Grooming horses, riding them, and helping them foal were all a natural part of Beryl's upbringing. She had little formal schooling. Her friends were the children of her father's African employees. From them she learned to speak Swahili, Nandi, and Masai, and went along on hunting expeditions, setting out at dawn. Barefooted and armed with spears, Beryl and her friends would hunt for wildebeest, antelope, warthogs, and other animals all day. At her side was always Puller, her beloved dog.

When she was seventeen, her father lost his farm and left Kenya to start a new business. But Beryl stayed on, supporting herself as a racehorse trainer. Years later, at age twenty-eight, after an early marriage that ended in divorce, she became the first woman in Africa to obtain a commercial flying license. Covering areas that had not yet been surveyed, and landing in places that were often no more than hastily cleared strips in the bush, she flew mail, medicine, and sometimes passengers all across East Africa. To facilitate elephant hunts, she began scouting elephants by air—a dangerous and lucrative business that she eventually abandoned. It was absurd, she came to believe, for a man to kill an elephant.

In 1936, Beryl flew from Nairobi to London, a route she had flown several

times. She was now an experienced pilot, with some 250,000 flying miles to her credit. At a dinner party held by John Carberry, a rich aristocrat she knew from Nairobi, one of the guests leaned across the table and said, "J. C., why don't you finance Beryl for a record flight?" From there the conversation turned to one of the few distances not yet covered: England to America, east to west. "Want to chance it?" asked Carberry. "Yes," answered Beryl.

A plane was commissioned for the flight and, for the next three months, Beryl watched every step of its construction. It was a Percival Gull, a top-of-the-line sports plane used in races, modified and strengthened to carry the weight of extra fuel. To increase the Gull's range from 660 to 3,600 miles, supplementary fuel tanks were installed throughout the plane. Each tank had to run out of gas before the next could be used, which meant that the engine might die for a few seconds, leaving the aircraft without power in midflight. As departure drew closer, Beryl had second thoughts. Feeling "much less brave than foolhardy," she told herself that there was still time to back out, knowing at the same time that "nothing is so inexorable as a promise to your pride."

It was September 4. The Gull stood ready, long and sleek, with a turquoise body and silver wings. As Beryl climbed into the cockpit, one of her ground crew, a Scottish mechanic, bestowed upon her the blessings of his country by giving her a sprig of heather. Another man had already lent her his watch with the comment, "Don't lose it, and for God's sake don't get it wet. Salt water would ruin the works."

This was a moment she had both dreaded and desired. She was off.

At first the Gull rebelled against its immense load of fuel. But then, with "the persuasion of stick and elevators, the dogmatic argument of blueprints that said that she had to fly because the figures proved it," the Gull lifted and was airborne.

After passing the Berehaven Lighthouse, Beryl flew in total darkness, on instruments alone. The roar of the plane, at first deafening, became a heavy, comforting drone. Hours passed. She now flew in a forty-mile head wind. How many flying hours were left? She could not be sure. Sixteen, maybe eighteen? She was waiting for one of the fuel tanks to run dry. When it did, and the engine sputtered and died, the sudden silence stunned her. As the plane fell from 2,000 to 1,000 feet, Beryl felt no fear, observing "with a kind of stupid disinterest" that her hands were "violently busy." Finding the switch for the next tank, she turned it and waited, hypnotized by the whirling needle of the altimeter. Three hundred feet and still no power. The sea was about to engulf her when, all of a sudden, the engine exploded back to life.

By daybreak, Beryl had flown blind for nineteen hours. She was tired and cold, but as the weather cleared and she sighted Newfoundland, her spirits rose. A few more hours and she would be in New York! She was approaching Cape Breton when the engine, now running on nearly a full tank of gas, once again conked out and died. Coughing and spluttering, it came back once, then stopped for good. For a few seconds, the Gull hung on "a motionless propeller," then nose-dived toward the island below. On impact, Beryl was thrown forward, shattering the cockpit window. Bleeding from a cut on her head, she stumbled out of the plane and sank knee-deep into muck. She glanced at the borrowed watch, noting, "Twenty-four hours and twenty-five minutes, Atlantic flight. Abingdon, England, to a nameless swamp—nonstop."

A fisherman saw the Gull's tail sticking up in the air and came to Beryl's rescue. Apart from the head wound, she was unharmed. Her first concern: to find a telephone so that she could let her friends know that she was still alive and prevent a needless search. On the following day, she flew to New York in another aircraft and received a hero's welcome. It was later discovered that ice had lodged in the air intake of the last fuel tank. By all accounts, she should have crashed long before reaching land.

The flight made Beryl famous. For several years she lived in California, where she wrote her autobiography, *West with the Night*. She never attempted another record flight. Instead she returned to Kenya, becoming one of the country's most successful racehorse trainers. She died in 1986, only a few weeks before the fiftieth anniversary of that long, dark night when she made it solo the hard way, east to west, across the North Atlantic.

"WRONG WAY" CORRIGAN

*W*here am I?"

The smiling young pilot was apparently nonplussed. He had landed in Ireland at Dublin's airport without a permit—or even a passport—and was now confronting several frowning customs officers.

"I took off from New York early Sunday with the intention of flying to Los Angeles," he explained. "After twenty-six hours without a stop, I decided to come down through the clouds. I was puzzled to see water, since I figured I couldn't have reached the Pacific yet. I must have misread my compass and followed the wrong end of the needle."

The Irish, never averse to a good yarn, took another look at his primitive plane and cheered him for his audacity. And when word of his remarkable flight reached the United States, the pilot, Douglas Corrigan, promptly became known as "Wrong Way" Corrigan.

44

The story of Douglas Corrigan, an Irish-American mechanic, has been called an Irish fairy tale, an impish yarn spun with a straight face. It unfolded in 1938 but really began eleven years earlier. Corrigan was then twenty, living in San Diego and working as part of the team that built *The Spirit of St. Louis,* the plane Charles Lindbergh flew solo across the Atlantic in 1927. Hearing that Lindbergh had safely landed in Paris, Corrigan joined his coworkers in a wild car ride through the streets, waving and shouting. Lindbergh was Corrigan's hero. Someday, Corrigan hoped, he too would make that same transatlantic flight.

Yet it seemed a remote possibility. Corrigan was just an ordinary guy, struggling to make ends meet, and, like many others, bitten by the aviation bug. Still, in 1927, Corrigan managed to get a pilot's license and began flying in his spare time. He became a barnstormer, renting airplanes whenever he could. In 1931, despite the Depression, he had saved enough money to buy a plane of his own. It was a battered old machine, but Corrigan fell in love with it, slept in it, fussed over it, and, to make a few extra dollars, carried passengers in it. Then, working toward his dream of duplicating his hero's transatlantic flight, he replaced three of the plane's four seats with fuel tanks, installed a stronger engine, and, to test his navigational skills, made several cross-country trips. He was set to go—except for one major obstacle: new, more stringent regulations, especially for trips overseas.

During the 1930s, airplanes had become faster, sleeker, and more powerful. Aviation was turning into big business. Corrigan, with his old "crate" of a plane

and pioneering spirit, was bound to run into difficulty. In 1937 he applied for a government permit to fly from New York to London, but because his plane was nearly ten years old, he was turned down. Next year, a federal inspector begrudgingly granted him a license for a nonstop flight from Los Angeles to New York—and back, if everything went well. So, on July 8, 1938, Corrigan took off from Los Angeles, arriving in New York twenty-seven hours later with exactly four gallons of gasoline to spare. Nine days later, on the 17th, he was ready to return to Los Angeles. A handful of people saw him take off, wondering why he headed northeast instead of west toward the Pacific Coast.

After arriving in Ireland, Corrigan offered an explanation for what had happened. Early on during the flight, he said, the clouds had parted, revealing a city he had assumed to be Baltimore. Now he realized that it must have been Boston. If only the compass hadn't pointed him in the wrong direction. . . .

For a few weeks, the world laughed. It had found an unlikely hero, a courageous, mirthful individual who thumbed his nose at authority. For once, government officials displayed a sense of humor. His pilot's license was suspended, but only until the day he returned to New York—by ship.

There Corrigan was treated to a ticker-tape parade on Broadway. A nationwide tour followed. He went to the White House to meet with President Roosevelt, received membership in the Liars' Club of Burlington, Wisconsin, and was hailed "Chief Wrong Way" by a Native American tribe in Tulsa, Oklahoma. Everywhere he visited, he was showered with compasses, and Abilene, Texas, presented him with a watch that ran backward.

Corrigan eventually retired to California for a comfortable long life on a citrus farm. Asked about his flight and the commotion it caused, his response was always the same: a mischievous grin and "Man, I didn't mean to do this at all."

Bibliography

Joseph-Michel and Jacques-Étienne Montgolfier 1740–1810, 1745-1799
Gillispie, Charles C. *The Montgolfier Brothers and the Invention of Aviation, 1783–1784.* Princeton, NJ: Princeton University Press, 1983.

Alberto Santos-Dumont 1873–1932
Brown, Rose (Johnston). *Bicycle in the Sky: The Story of Alberto Santos-Dumont.* New York: Charles Scribner's Sons, 1953.
Winters, Nancy. *Man Flies: The Story of Alberto Santos-Dumont, Master of the Balloon, Conqueror of the Air.* Hopewell, NJ: The Ecco Press, 1997.

Calbraith (Cal) Perry Rodgers 1879–1912
Lebow, Eileen F. *Cal Rodgers and the* Vin Fiz: *The First Transcontinental Flight.* Washington and London: Smithsonian Institution Press, 1989.
Saban, Vera. "Cal Rodgers from the Atlantic to the Pacific." *Aviation Quarterly,* vol. 6, no. 4, 1980.
Stein, E. P. *Flight of the* Vin Fiz. New York: Arbor House, 1985.

Bessie Coleman 1892–1926
Hart, Philip S. *Up in the Air: The Story of Bessie Coleman.* Minneapolis: Carolrhoda Books, 1996.
Rich, Doris L. *Queen Bess: Daredevil Aviator.* Washington and London: Smithsonian Institution Press, 1993.

James (Jimmy) H. Doolittle 1896–1993
Glines, Carroll V. *Jimmy Doolittle: Daredevil Aviator and Scientist.* New York: The Macmillan Company, 1972.

Beryl Markham 1902–1986
Markham, Beryl. *West with the Night.* San Francisco: North Point Press, 1983.
Trzebinski, Errol. *The Lives of Beryl Markham.* New York and London: W. W. Norton & Company, 1993.

Douglas ("Wrong Way") Corrigan 1907–1995
Corrigan, Douglas. *That's My Story.* New York: E. P. Dutton & Company, 1938.

OTHER BOOKS
Ault, Phil. *By the Seat of Their Pants.* New York: Dodd, Mead & Company, 1978.
Aymar, Brandt, ed. *Men in the Air: The Best Flight Stories of All Time from Greek Mythology to the Space Age.* New York: Crown Publishers, 1990.
Becker, Beril. *Dreams and Realities of the Conquest of the Skies.* New York: Simon & Schuster, 1970.
Harris, Sherwood. *The First to Fly: Aviation's Pioneer Days.* New York: Simon & Schuster, 1970.
Howard, Fred. *Wilbur and Orville: A Biography of the Wright Brothers.* New York: Alfred A. Knopf, 1987.
Jablonski, Edward. *Man with Wings: A Pictorial History of Aviation.* New York: Doubleday, 1980.
Moolman, Valerie. *The Road to Kitty Hawk.* Alexandria, VA: Time-Life Books, 1980.
Nevin, David. *The Pathfinders.* Alexandria, VA: Time-Life Books, 1980.
Taylor, John W. R. and Kenneth Munson. *History of Aviation.* New York: Crown Publishers, 1975.
Taylor, John W. R., et al. *The Lore of Flight.* Gothenburg, Sweden: AB Nordbok, 1971 (New York: Barnes & Noble Books, 1996).